This book
belongs to

Published in the UK by Sweet Cherry Publishing Limited, 2024
Unit 36, Vulcan House, Vulcan Road, Leicester, LE5 3EF, United Kingdom

Unit 31, The Pottery, Bakers Point,
Pottery Road, Dún Laoghaire,
Dublin A96 EV18, Ireland

2 4 6 8 10 9 7 5 3 1

ISBN: 978-1-80263-548-5

Colourblocks Annual 2025

www.sweetcherrypublishing.com

Printed and bound in China

COLOUR
BLOCKS
OFFICIAL
ANNUAL
2025

Contents

Red

All about Red

Red loves: adventures and discovering new things!

Fun fact: Red was the first Colourblock in Colourland.

You can see red in:

tomatoes

strawberries

fire engines

Can you colour in Red?

Search for red

Can you find all the red things in this picture?
Circle each one when you find it.

How many red things did you find?

Answers on page 66

Let's colour!

Colour the big bus in red!

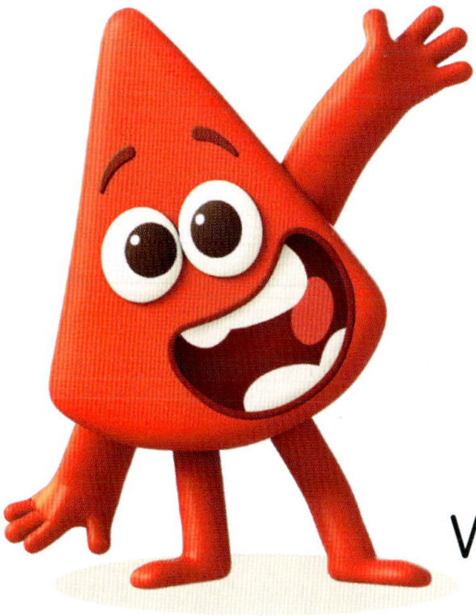

Odd one out

Answers on page 66

Circle the odd one out.
Which picture is NOT red?

ACTIVITY

Orange

I am Orange. I am full of energy!

All about Orange

Orange loves:
dancing, playing and any sort of exercise!

Fun fact:
Orange's favourite drink is orange juice.

You can see orange in:

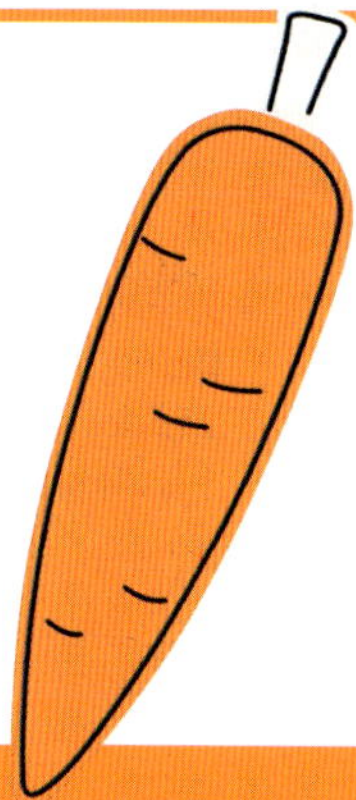

carrots

pumpkins

tigers

Can you colour in Orange?

Dotty pumpkin

Follow the dots to draw the pumpkin.
Then colour it in and draw on a silly face!

Answers on page 66

Maze play

Answers on page 66

Orange is playing basketball. Help her get the ball through the maze and into the net.

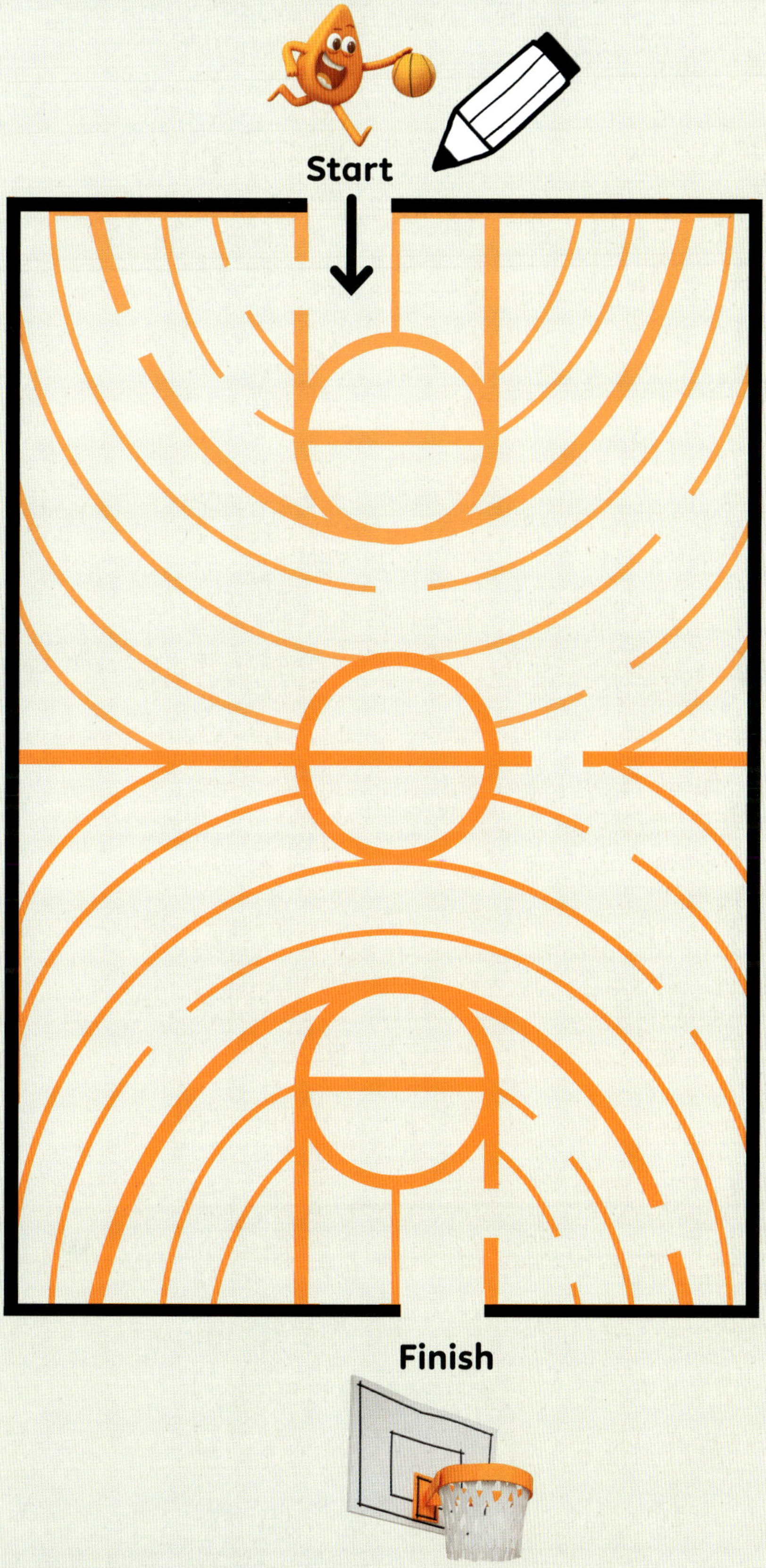

Yellow

All about Yellow

Yellow loves:
colour parties and having fun!

Fun fact:
Yellow loves his rubber ducks!

Meet the rest of the Printing Crew on page 56!

You can see yellow in:

bananas

bumble bees

sunflowers

Can you colour in Yellow?

Colour the blanks

Finish the picture by colouring the blank shapes in yellow.

Answers on page 66

Lime

All about Lime

Lime loves:
singing, dancing and rollerskating!

Fun fact:
Lime loves performing and being in the limelight!

You can see lime in:

limes

Can you colour in Lime?

Green

I am Green. I am the colour of living things!

All about Green

Green loves:
plants, animals and helping her friends!

Fun fact:
Green likes to talk to animals.

Can you colour in Green?

You can see green in:

pears

frogs

trees

Pattern match

Look at the patterns below. Can you make the patterns on the right match by colouring in the blank shapes?

1.

2.

3.

Answers on page 66.

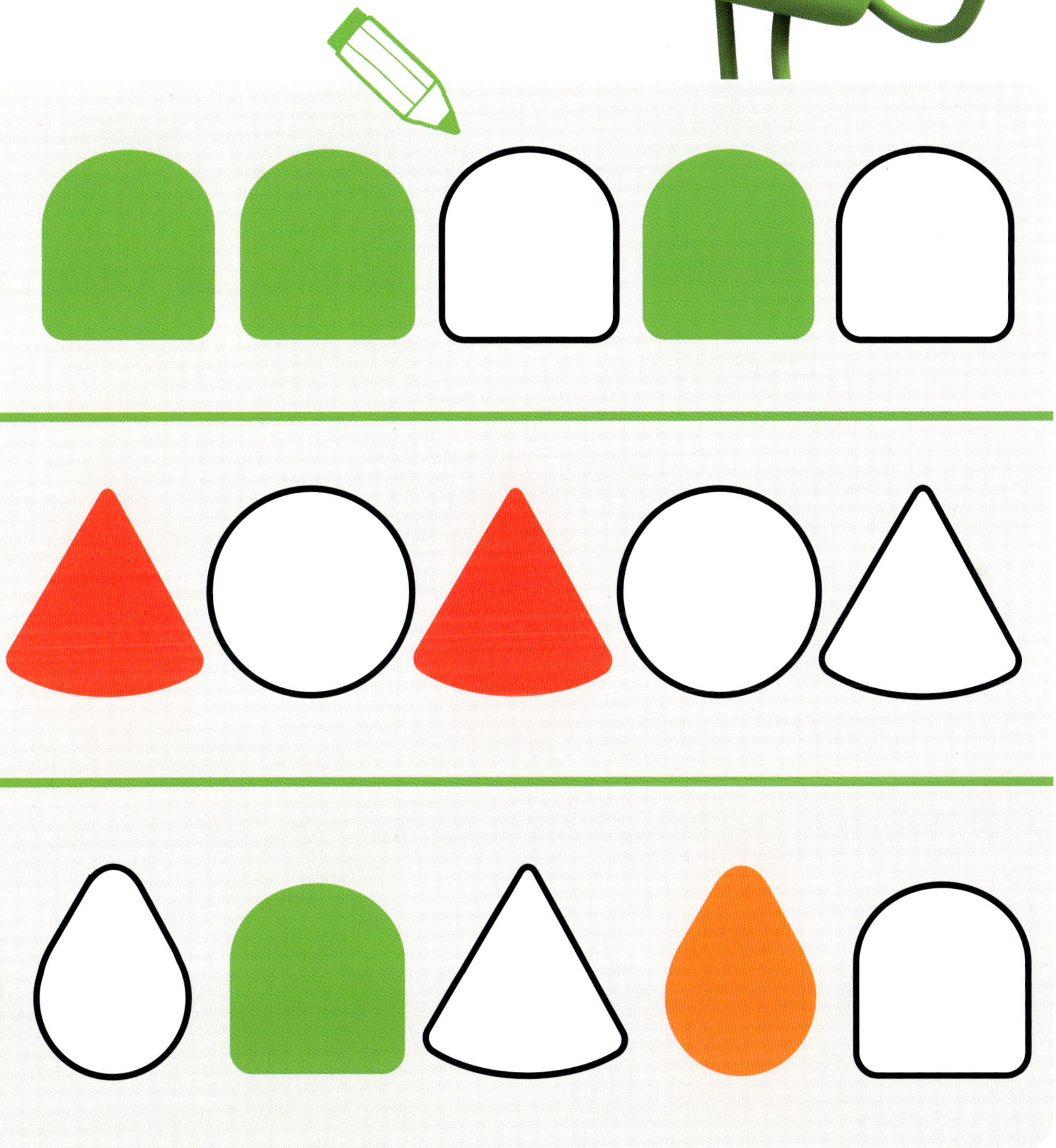

1.

2.

3.

ACTIVITY

Doodles

Follow the dots to doodle with the Colourblocks.

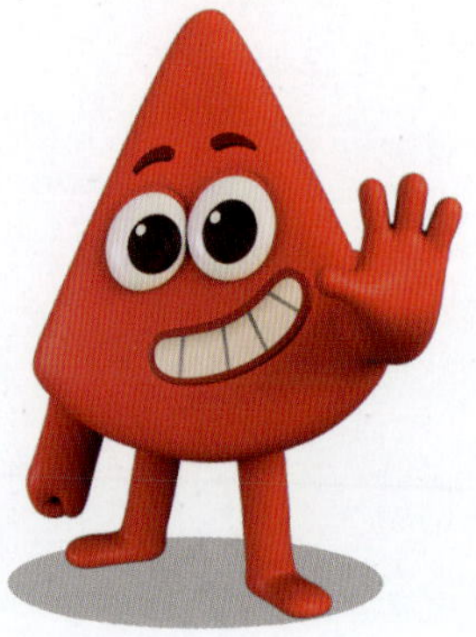

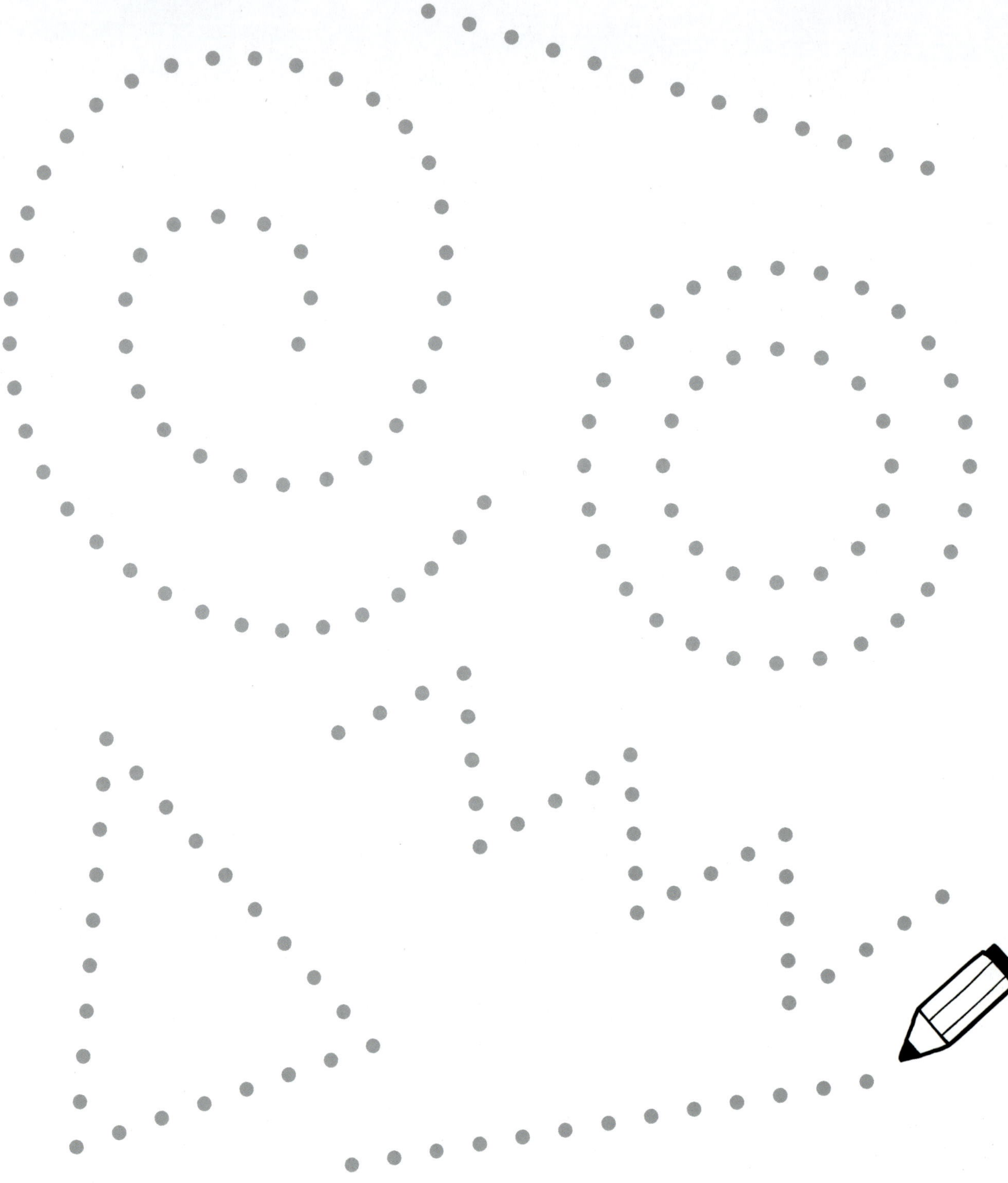

Let's get creative!

Blue

I am Blue.
Cool to
meet you!

All about Blue

Blue loves: blueberries, boats and sailing across the sea!

Fun fact: Blue likes to go swimming.

You can see blue in:

blueberries

whales

bluebirds

Can you colour in Blue?

Beautiful blues

Meet Blue's friends: Sky Blue and Deep Blue! Dive into the big blue sea with them to spot all the things in the list. Tick each one when you spot it.

Answers on page 66

Sky Blue

I am
Sky Blue.
I love to fly
through the
sky blue
sky!

Deep Blue

I am
Deep Blue.
I love diving
into the deep
blue sea!

Indigo

Fun fact:

Indigo is like blue, but a bit more purple!

Can you colour in Indigo's boots?

I am Indigo. I am a Rainbow Chaser!

Violet

I am Violet.
I am a Rainbow
Chaser too!

Fun fact:

Violet is like purple,
but a bit more blue!

Can you colour in Violet's book?

Rainbow mix-up

The Colourblocks have been painting rainbows, but some of them are mixed up! Tick the rainbows that have the right colours. Put a cross under the rainbows that do not.

Example:

Clue: Look at the example and read the rhyme to help.

We're colouring a rainbow. Make it bold and bright.
Just paint seven colours. And get the order right...

First **Red**,
Then **Orange**.
Next add **Yellow**,
Green,
Blue,
Indigo,
Violet,
And there's a rainbow, just for you!

Scan the code to hear the song!

Answers on page 67

Purple

All about Purple

Purple loves: making patterns, playing games and using his imagination!

Fun fact: Purple lives in a royal purple castle!

You can see purple in:

cabbages

plums

aubergines

Can you colour in Purple?

Little Red Riding Hood

2

Little Red Riding Hood packs her basket full of party things, to take to her grandma's house.

STORY

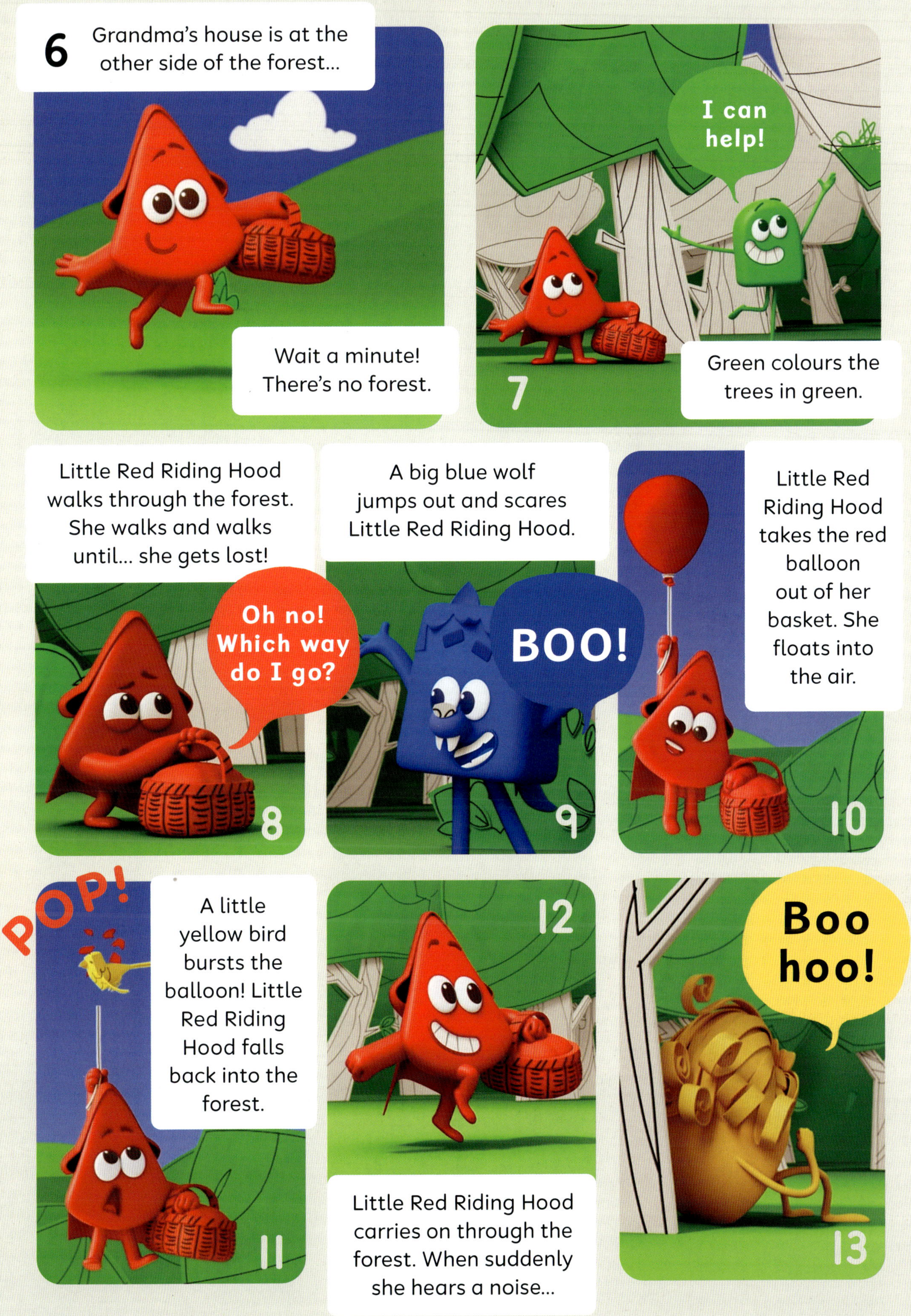
6
Grandma's house is at the other side of the forest...
Wait a minute! There's no forest.
I can help!
7
Green colours the trees in green.
Little Red Riding Hood walks through the forest. She walks and walks until... she gets lost!
Oh no! Which way do I go?
8
A big blue wolf jumps out and scares Little Red Riding Hood.
BOO!
9
Little Red Riding Hood takes the red balloon out of her basket. She floats into the air.
10
POP!
A little yellow bird bursts the balloon! Little Red Riding Hood falls back into the forest.
11
12
Little Red Riding Hood carries on through the forest. When suddenly she hears a noise...
Boo hoo!
13

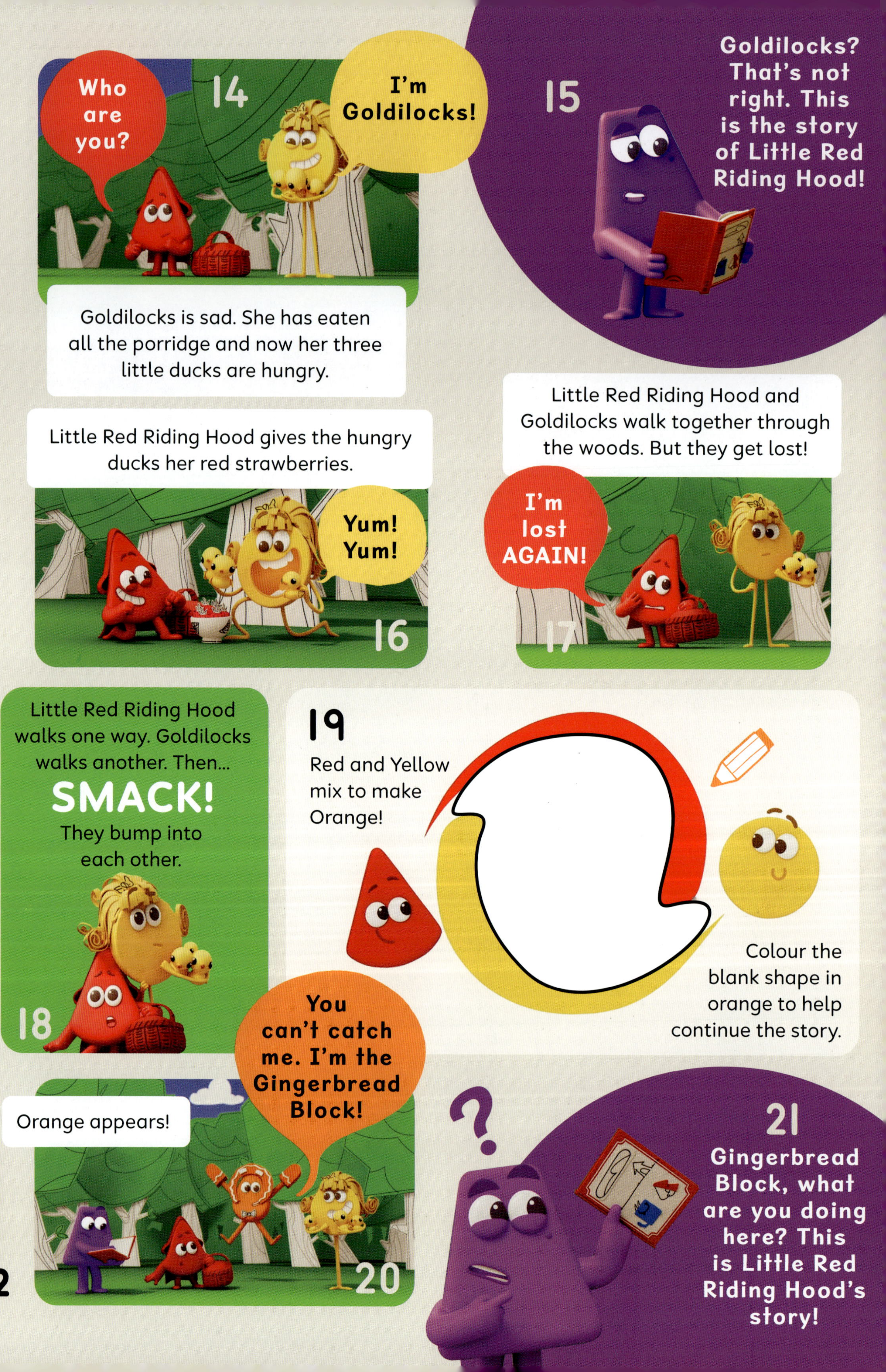
14
Who are you?
I'm Goldilocks!
15
Goldilocks? That's not right. This is the story of Little Red Riding Hood!
Goldilocks is sad. She has eaten all the porridge and now her three little ducks are hungry.
Little Red Riding Hood gives the hungry ducks her red strawberries.
Yum! Yum!
16
Little Red Riding Hood and Goldilocks walk together through the woods. But they get lost!
I'm lost AGAIN!
17
Little Red Riding Hood walks one way. Goldilocks walks another. Then...
SMACK!
They bump into each other.
18
19
Red and Yellow mix to make Orange!
Colour the blank shape in orange to help continue the story.
Orange appears!
You can't catch me. I'm the Gingerbread Block!
20
21
Gingerbread Block, what are you doing here? This is Little Red Riding Hood's story!

The Gingerbread Block knows the way to Grandma's house.
Follow me!
22
23
The Colourblocks arrive at Grandma's house, to find... a big blue wolf!
Big blue wolf, did you eat Grandma?
No. I don't eat grandmas, I eat blueberries!
Then where is Grandma?
24
I'm here!
25
26
Little Red Riding Hood looks in her basket, to find the party things. The balloon popped... the strawberries were eaten... and now the cake is missing!
Oh no!
27
Little Red Riding Hood is sad. How can Grandma have a party now?
Come here, Little Red Riding Hood!
This is the most colourful party EVER!
28
The Colourblocks have made a party for Grandma! There are oranges, yellow cake, blueberries and green decorations.
29
And they all live happily ever after!
43

Answers on pages 66

Fun flowers

Follow the dots to draw the flowers, then colour them in.

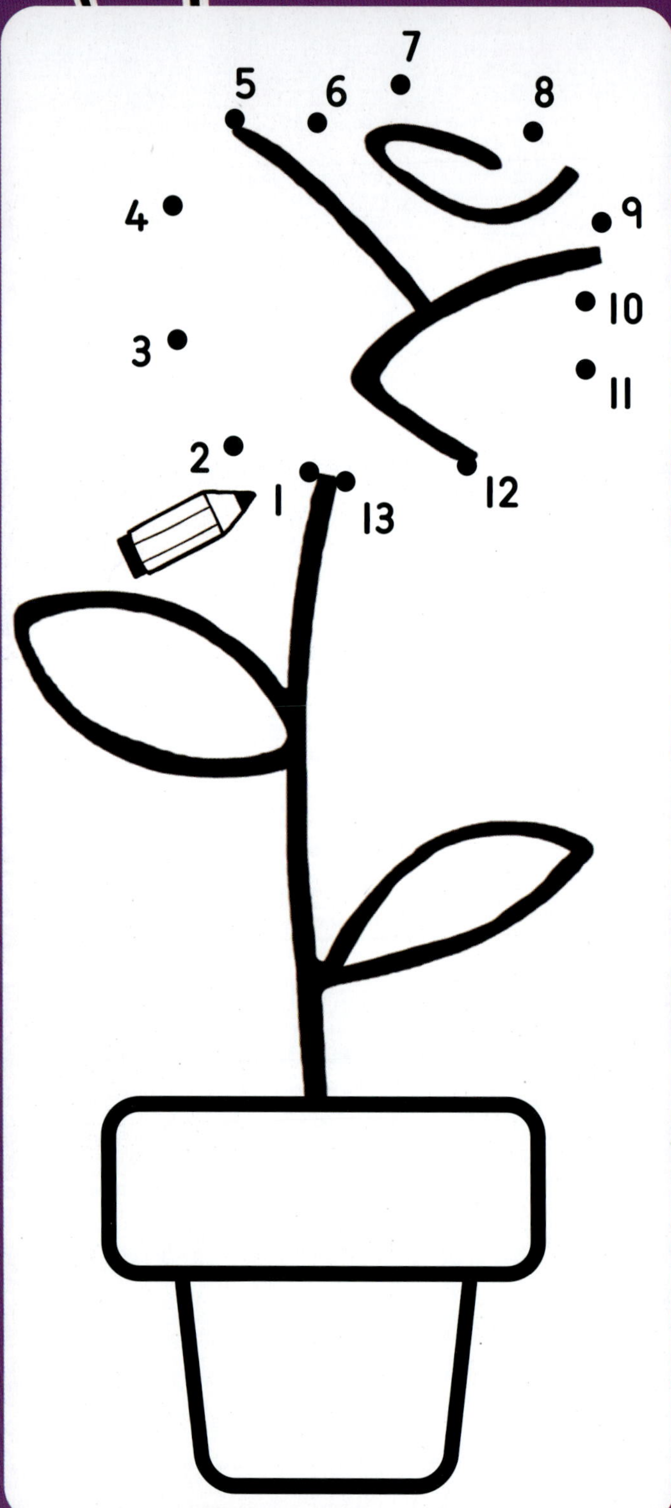

I spy... purple!

Answers on pages 67

Let's play 'I Spy'!
What has Purple seen? Read the clues and then find the things in the picture.

Something purple that you unwrap on your birthday!

Something purple that you swing on!

A big purple building, where kings live!

Who's hiding?

The Colourblocks are playing hide-and-seek. Who's hiding? Read the speech bubbles and fill in the gaps.

ACTIVITY

Answers on page 67

I am Purple.

I am Lime.

I am Yellow.

I am Orange.

Black, White and Grey match

Meet Black, White and Grey!
They have been collecting their favourite things.
Draw lines to match the item to the Colourblock that is the same colour.

Answers on page 67

ACTIVITY

Pink

Fun fact:

Pink is a mix of red and white.

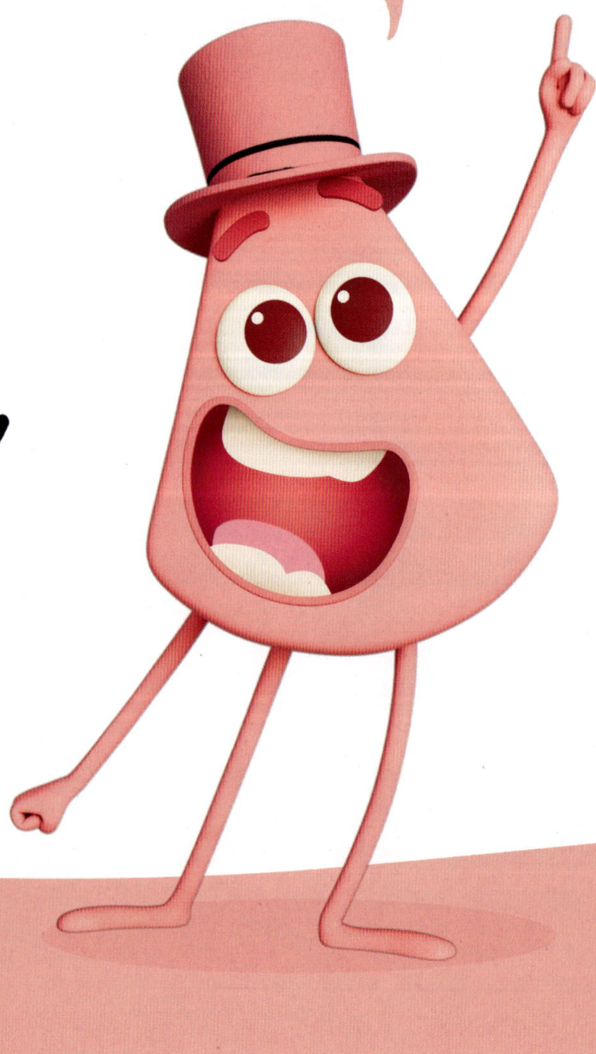

Can you colour in Pink's pretty shell?

Brown

Fun fact:

Lots of colour mixes make Brown!

I am Brown. I like exploring!

Can you colour in Brown's owl friend?

Rubber duck race

Can you help Yellow lead all the rubber ducks back to the pond?

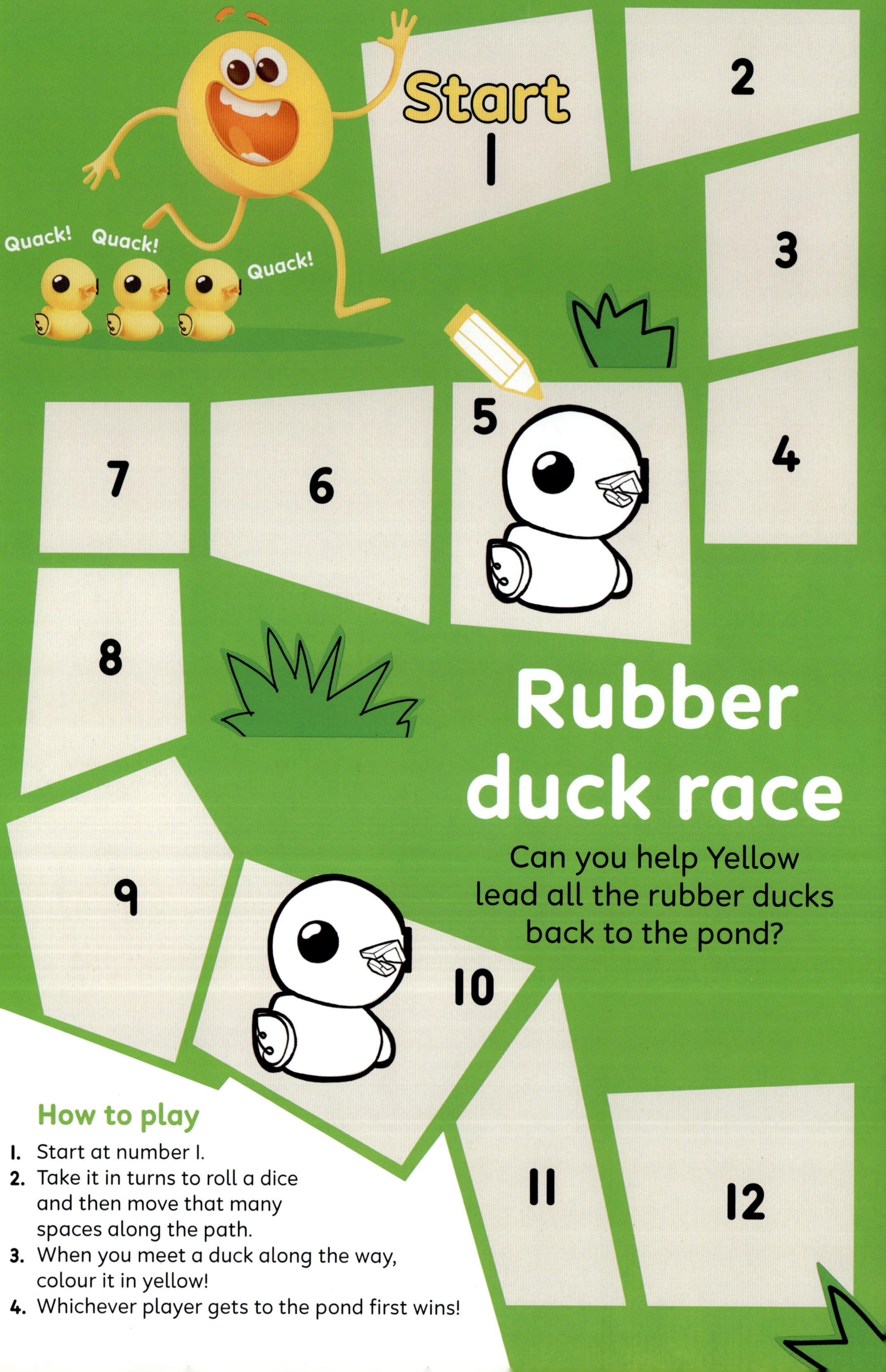

How to play

1. Start at number 1.
2. Take it in turns to roll a dice and then move that many spaces along the path.
3. When you meet a duck along the way, colour it in yellow!
4. Whichever player gets to the pond first wins!

18
19
20
17
21
Finish
22
16
Play by yourself or with a friend!
15
13
14

Name that colour!

Time for a quiz!
Can you answer these colour questions?
Tick the right answers.

1.

Which apple is red?

2.

Which colour does this mix make?

3.

Which Colourblock is the happiest colour in Colourland?

Answers on page 67

4.

Which gem is blue?

5.

Which Colourblock is a Rainbow Chaser?

6.

Which balloon is yellow?

Answers on page 67

Meet the Printing Crew!

Say hello to the Printing Crew!
They have got their cartridge cars mixed up.
Can you draw a line to lead each Colourblock to their car?

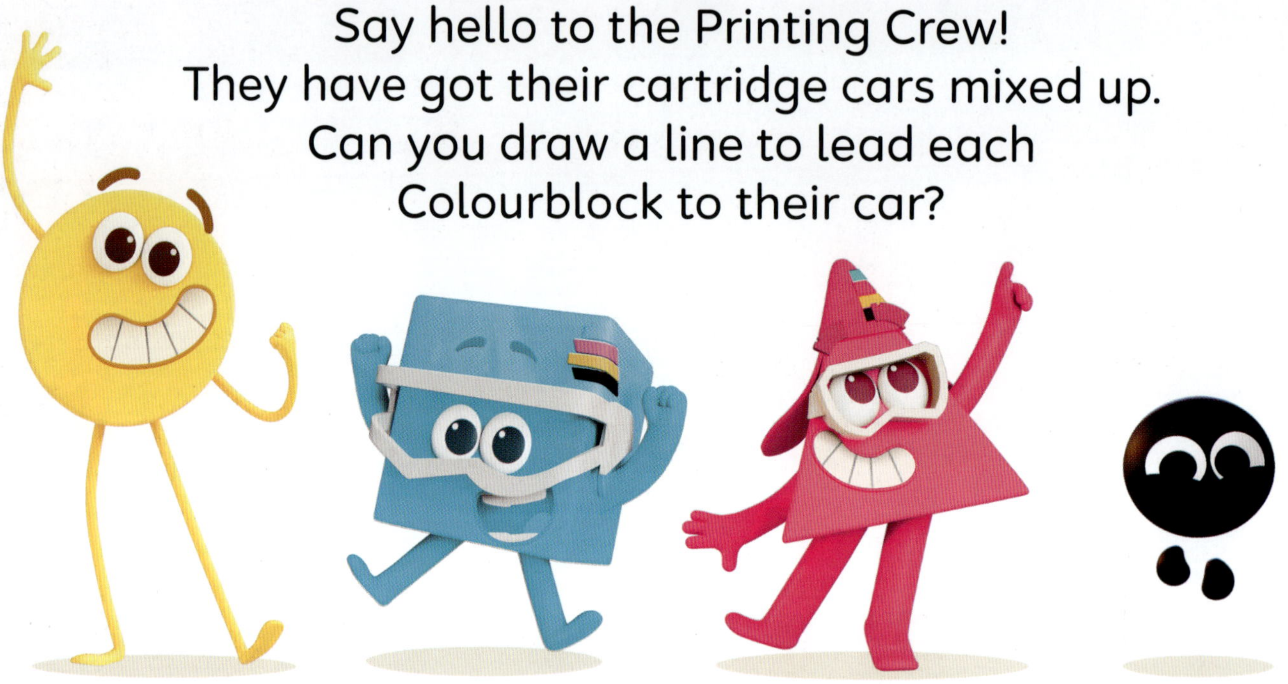

Yellow **Cyan** **Magenta** **Black**

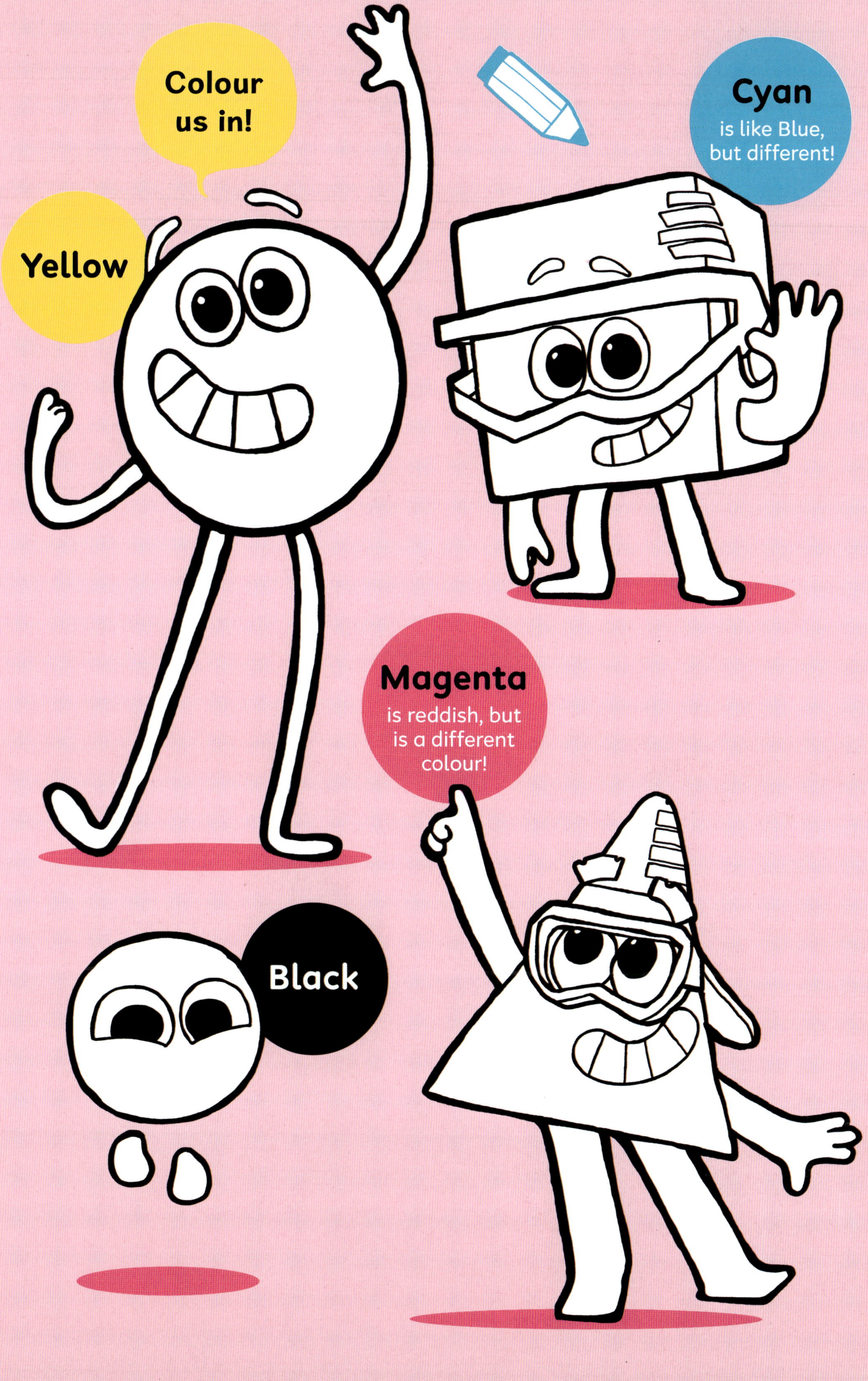
Colour us in!
Yellow
Cyan is like Blue, but different!
Magenta is reddish, but is a different colour!
Black

The Mixing Factory

2 **Red** and **Yellow** walk up to the mixing machine. They touch the empty tubes and POP! The tubes turn **red** and **yellow**.

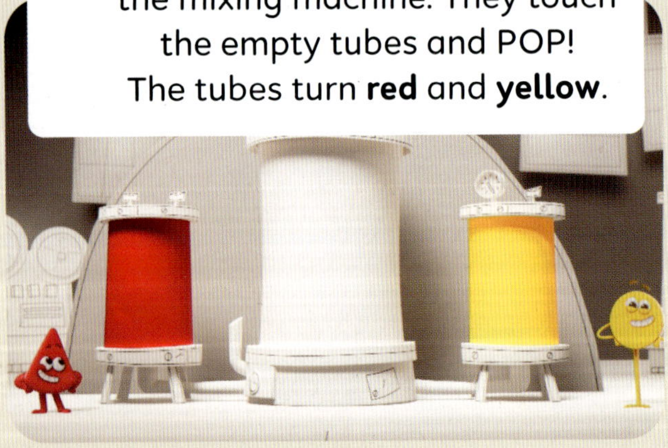

3 Now stir them round, what have you found?

4 Colour in **Orange**!

5 Next, it's **Blue** and **Yellow's** turn.

6 Let's stir them round, what have you found?

7 Colour in **Green**!

10

Now stir them round, what have you found?

11

Colour in **Purple**!

12 **Black** and **White** arrive at the Mixing Factory. What colour mixes can they make?

13

Take any colour and add White, you'll turn that colour pale - that's light!

 → 

Black has a different set of tricks, darkening colours when it's mixed.

 → 

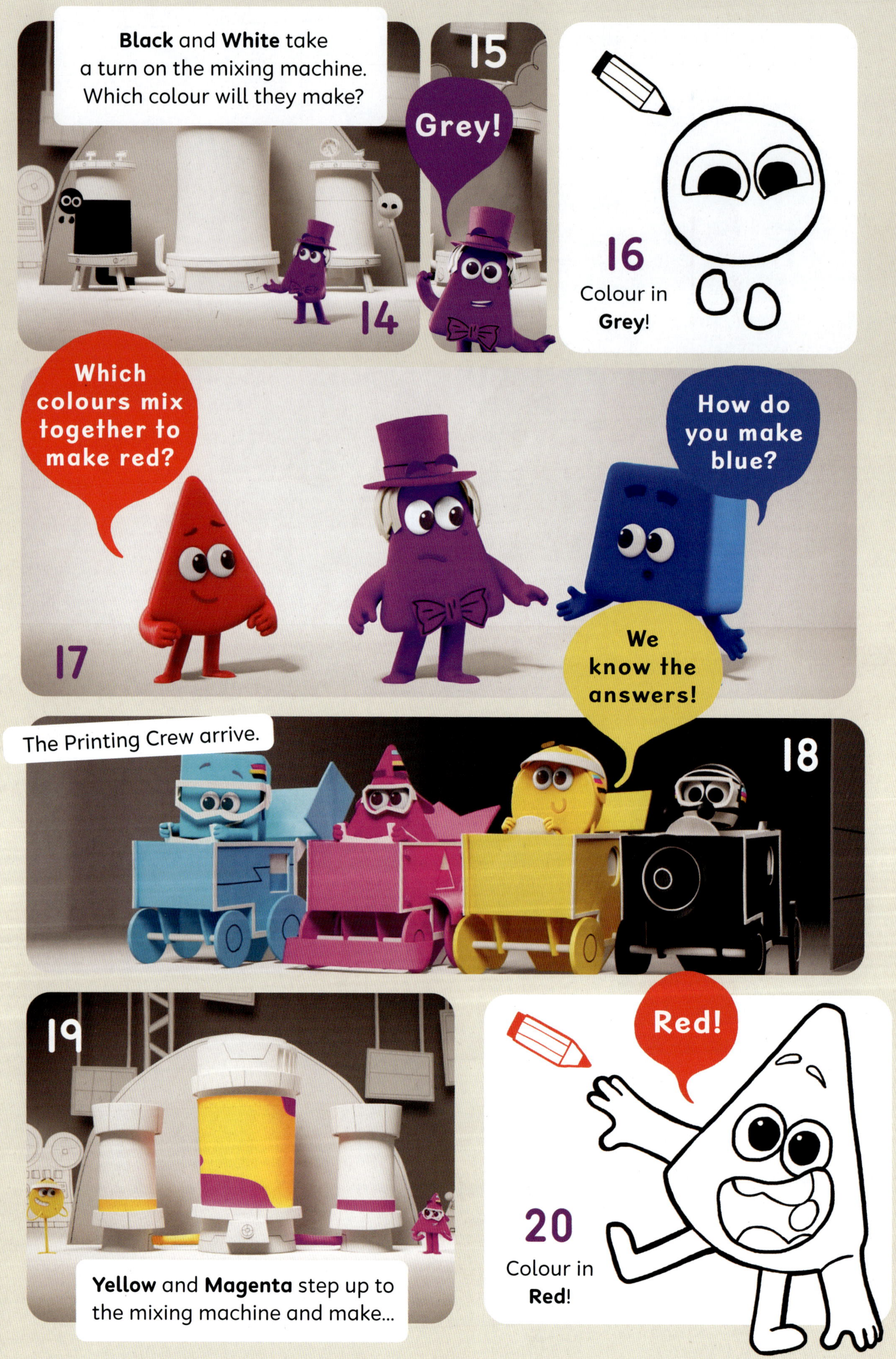
Black and White take a turn on the mixing machine. Which colour will they make?
14
15
Grey!
16
Colour in Grey!
Which colours mix together to make red?
How do you make blue?
17
We know the answers!
The Printing Crew arrive.
18
19
Yellow and Magenta step up to the mixing machine and make...
Red!
20
Colour in Red!

21 **Cyan** and **Magenta** take a turn on the mixing machine.

22
We'll mix a lot, what have we got?

Blue!

23
Colour in **Blue**!

24

25

You've watched our colour mixing.
We've put on quite a show.
Now it's your turn to mix it up,
Go on, give it a go!

Mix and match

Answers on page 67

Read The Mixing Factory story to help work out the answers (p58)!

Which colours do these mixes make?
Draw lines to lead each mix to the correct colour.

Now colour in the Colourblocks
to show who the mixes have made!

Magic colours show

Green is performing magic tricks!
Help her colour the balloons to show that adding white or black can make colours lighter or darker.

1.

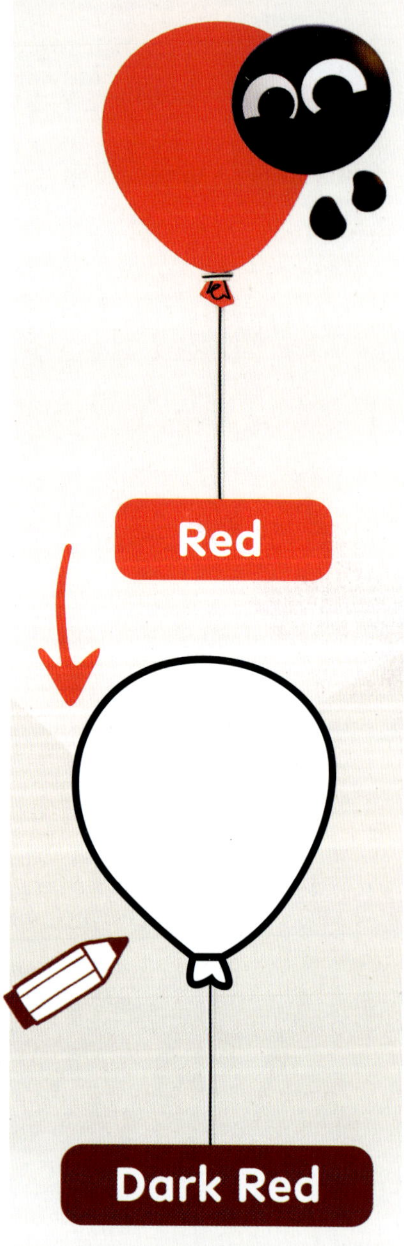

2.

Answers on page 67

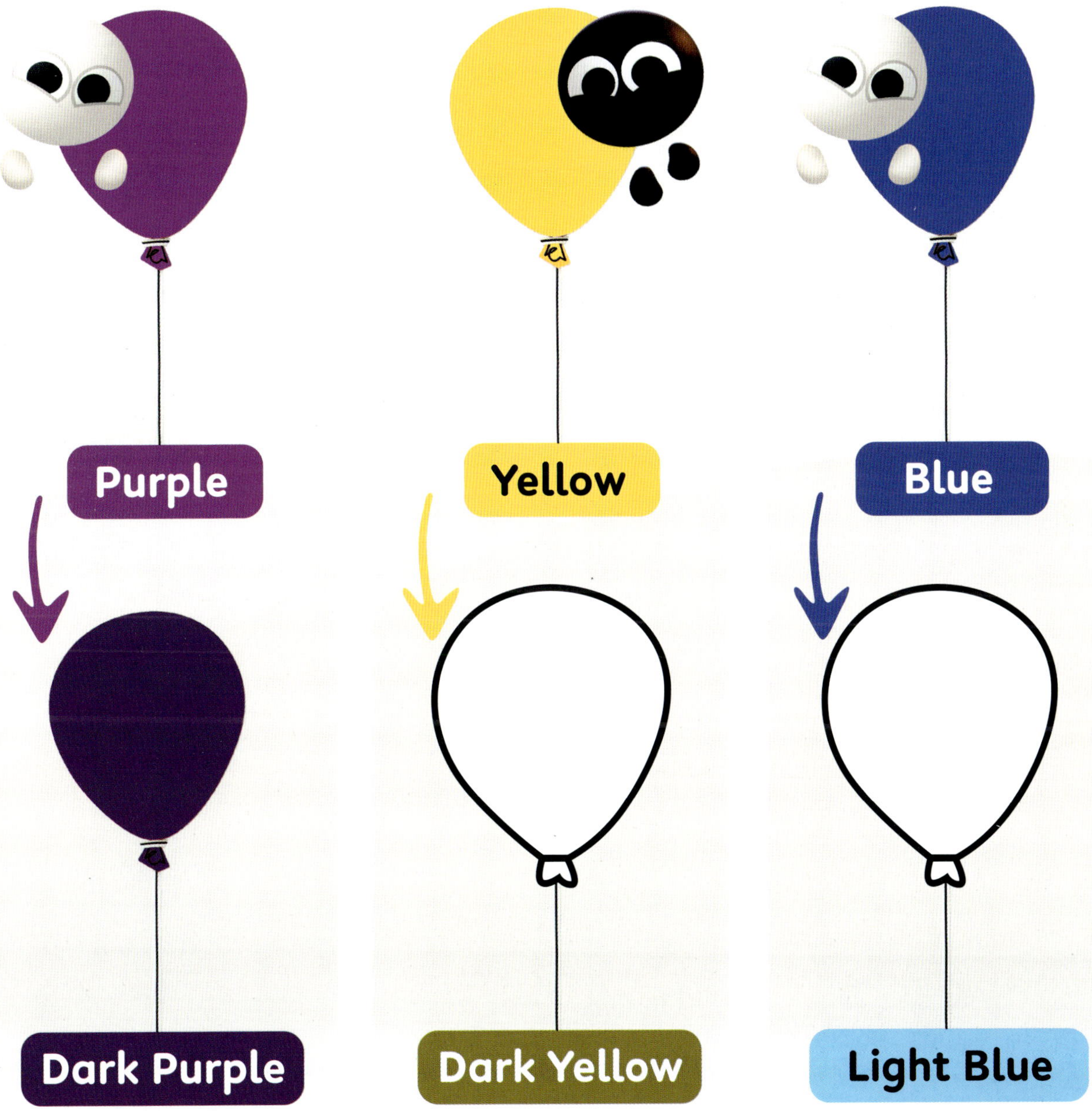

3.

4.

5.

Answers

Pages 10-11

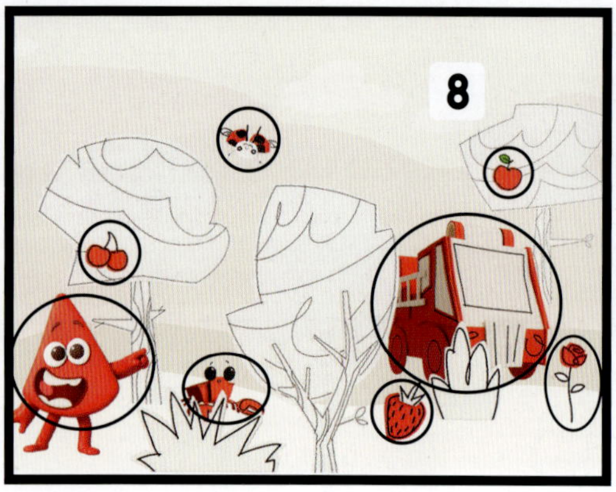

Page 13

Page 16

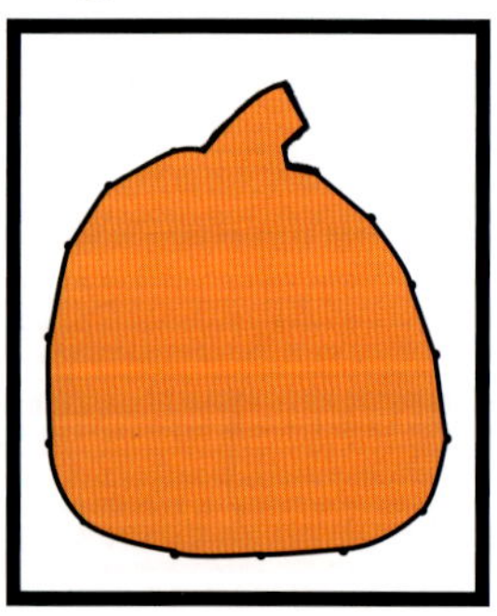

Page 17

Pages 20-21

Page 27

Pages 32-33

Page 37

Page 44

Page 45

Pages 46-47

Pages 48-49

Pages 54-55

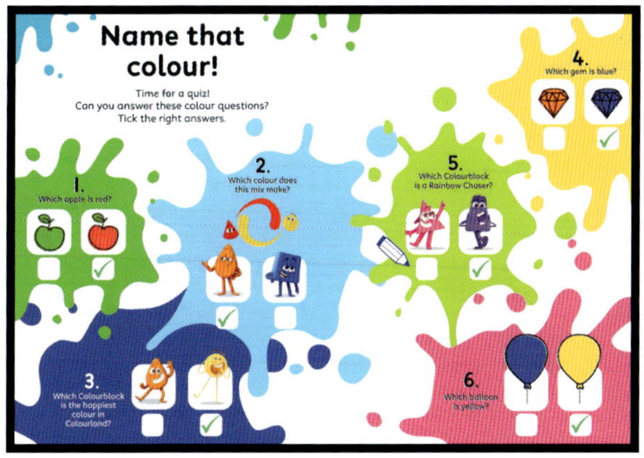

Page 56

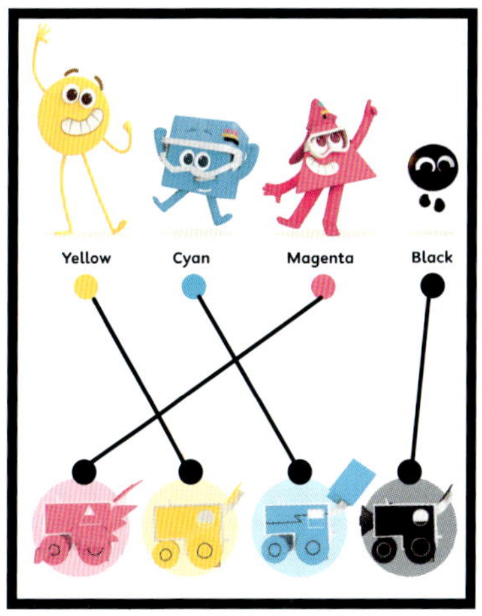

Page 62

Pages 64-65

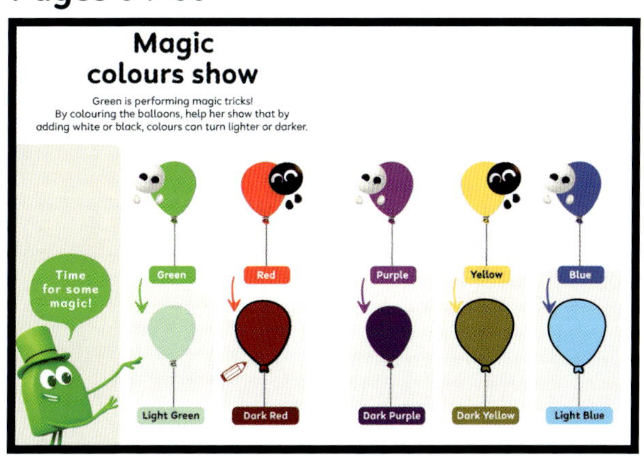

Well done,

Rainbow Chaser!